MY NAME IS A STORY

written by Ashanti

illustrated by Monica Mikai

HARPER

An Imprint of HarperCollins*Publishers*

Welcome to
Room 3!
TAKE HOME
MR. HADI
PASS
PASS
NURSE
Rose
Alex
Luís

I wanted my name to be easy.

Easy like funny faces and finger paint,

like dizzy friends spinning

on a merry-go-round,

like recess, sunshine,

and skipping rocks.

I wanted my name to be easy like playground giggles sneak between the trees.

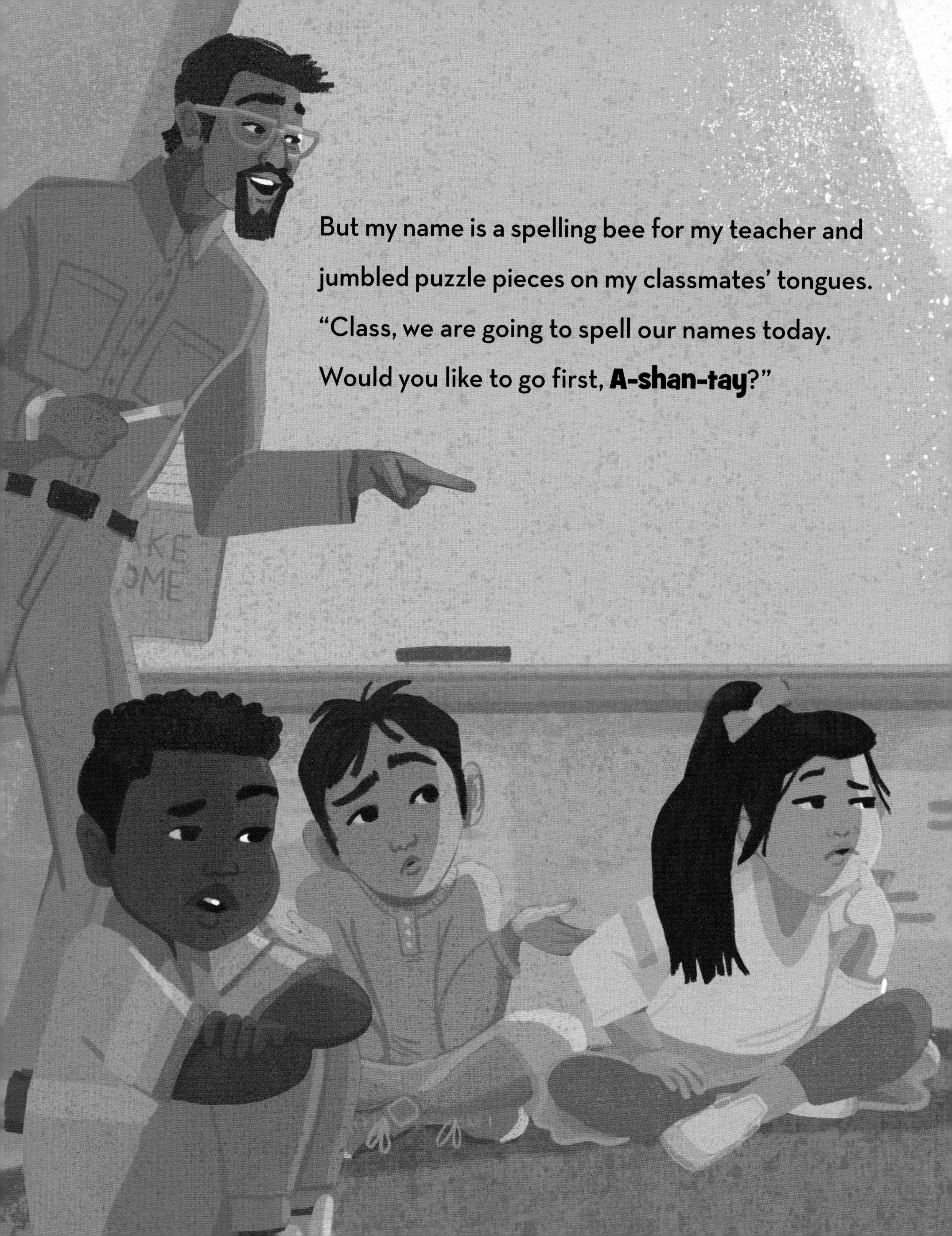

But my name is a spelling bee for my teacher and jumbled puzzle pieces on my classmates' tongues.

"Class, we are going to spell our names today. Would you like to go first, **A-shan-tay**?"

"**Ah-shoon-tee**? I've never heard of a name like that!"

"Hey, what kind of name is **A-shin-ty**?"

"And why does your name sound so *weird*?"

4
5
6
My name is
Ash
Homework:
Write your name!
TAKE
HOME

Too big.

Too hard.

Too much.

When I crawl into my mother's arms and my tears stain her favorite blouse, I explain that my name is an impossible maze.

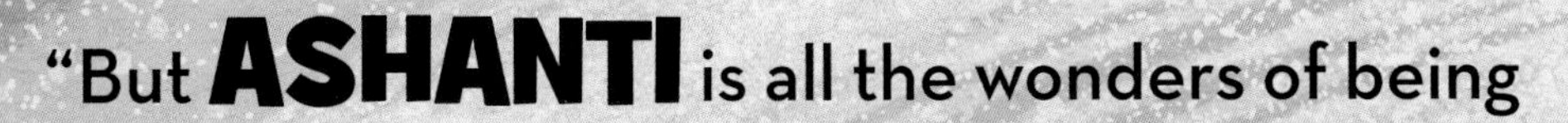

"But **ASHANTI** is all the wonders of being

AWESOME."

I look into Mama's warm eyes as she flips through each letter of my name like the pages of a cozy storybook.

"Ashanti is a thousand **SUNRISES**.

A kingdom on the golden **SHORES** of Ghana,

or busy city **SIDEWALKS**.

It's the **STRENGTH** of our people and our family."

“Is it Grandpa Jelani, whose name means **SMALL** but mighty?” I ask.

"Or Auntie Tina, who **SHINES** like a glistening river?"

"Yes, that's right, baby girl."

Mama grins as I breathe in deep.

"Ashanti is the rhythm of the **HAND GAMES** I play,

and the **HARMONY** in my songs."

“Ashanti’s the **ARC** of a double rainbow.

The **ART** in your sparkling eyes.

It is the smell of the sweetest **NECTARINE**,
and a **NIBBLE** of chocolate.

Ashanti is a **NIGHTTIME** star.”

I sit up straight and

wipe my tears.

I start to see.

"It's the winding

TWIST

in my dancing hips.

A **TINY** fib from
my mischievous lips."

A **TICKLE** monster.

“Ashanti is a great **IDEA**.

An **INSPIRATION!**

INNOVATION!

A bright **IMAGINATION!**" I shout.

Mama lifts my chin and wipes my cheeks.

"Ashanti is a big name for a girl with a big heart and big dreams."

"Your name is a story
to be read,
to be told,
and to be loved,
over and over again."

The very next day, I look my teacher in the eye and take my place in front of the classroom.

Hands on my hips and my head held high, I say,

"Easy like **APPLE PIE**

or as **STRONG**

as a **HIGH FIVE**.

My name is no mere **ACCESSORY**.

Saying my name with power is **NECESSARY**.

My name is a **TREASURE**

that is **INFINITE**."

LUNCH

“Never too big.
Never too hard.
And never, ever
too much.”

My name is

Ashanti.

My name is a story.

Sandeep

Makani

Rose

Itzel

Ash

Meena

Alex

Jen

WHAT'S YOURS?

Anika

Michael

anti

Lamont

Luís

MY MOTHER CAREFULLY PICKED OUT MY NAME: ASHANTI.

Ashanti can mean many things, like "thank you" or "woman of strength"; it is the name of an empire of people from Ghana who were courageous, loyal, and loving. It is not in the top one hundred names for babies, but it is a name that I am extremely proud of.

When I was young, I didn't know there was anything different about my name. It wasn't until I started going to school that I found that teachers and classmates struggled to pronounce it. Some would tease me, and others would try hard to get it right. Either way, I learned my name was different from everyone else's.

I asked my mother why she had given me such a difficult name. She sat me down and told me, "We picked your name out just for you. You are named after the strong women who came before you." She taught me to stand up for myself and to be proud to have such a unique and extraordinary name. I didn't get there overnight, but I learned how to love what was made just for me.

My Name Is a Story is a book for those kids with different names. Names that might be hard for some people to say or spell. Names that stick out during roll call. My hope is that readers understand every name is special and important and deserving of respect. Every name tells a little bit about where that person is from and who they are in the world.

MY NAME IS ASHANTI. WHAT'S YOURS?

To all the amazing children with unique names who have ever felt sad because their name was different. I hope you grow to love and appreciate the power and beauty in being extraordinary.

To my mom, a.k.a. the original Momanger, Tina Douglas; Stephan Dweck; Jerome Leventhal; Kirby Kim; William Archer; Richard Murphy; Michelle Huff; Gary Reichman; Robin Clark; Luana Kay Horry; Chelsea C. Donaldson; my dad, Ken-Kaide; and sister, Shia.

Finally, I would like to dedicate this book to my future child.
Yes! Your name will be unique and special too!

 For information address HarperCollins Children's Books, a division of HarperCollins Publishers, 195 Broadway, New York, NY 10007. • www.harpercollinschildrens.com • ISBN 978-0-06-322236-6
Typography by Chelsea C. Donaldson • 22 23 24 25 26 PC 10 9 8 7 6 5 4 3 2 1 ❖ First Edition